Daisy's Garden

Mordicai Gerstein 🎵 Susan Yard Harris

Hyperion Books for Children
New York

First Edition
1 3 5 7 9 10 8 6 4 2

Library of Congress Cataloging-in-Publication Data
Gerstein, Mordicai
Daisy's garden/Mordicai Gerstein and Susan Yard Harris—1st ed.
p.   cm.
Summary: A young girl and all the animals of the field come
together to plant and harvest a garden.
ISBN 0-7868-0096-8 (trade)—ISBN 0-7868-2080-2 (lib. bdg.)
[1. Gardening—Fiction.   2. Animals—Fiction.   3. Stories in
rhyme.]   I. Harris, Susan Yard.   II. Title.
PZ8.3.G327Dai   1995
[E]—dc20   94–22123

For Adi, with love

"IT'S APRIL!" says Daisy.
"The earth smells sweet,
like chocolate cake
beneath my feet.
The warm breeze tells me
spring has come.
Let's plant a
garden, everyone!

"A garden that we
all can share—
groundhog, rabbit,
skunk, and bear.
Field mice, crickets,
squirrel, and deer—
grab a hoe!
You're welcome here!"

"How can *I* help?"
asks the horse.
"Would you plow?"
"I would, of course!"

"What can *we* do?"
ask the moles.
"You can dig
some little holes."

The mice say,
"Everyone agrees,
we're the ones
to sow the seeds.

"Except a few
we'll save to munch,
in case we need
some snacks, or lunch."

The plump clouds sigh
as they float by.
"Your garden looks
a little dry."
First comes lightning.
Thunder crashes!
Everyone runs as
rain patters and splashes.

"I'll shine," says the sun as the sky turns blue. "I'll make plants grow and rainbows, too."

"IT'S MAY," says the cat.
"I'll smile and purr
and watch sprouts grow
while I lick my fur."

"I'll bark," says the dog,
"and welcome crows."
The crows say, "*Caw!*
We'll thin the rows."

"Some sprouts," says Daisy,
"are really weeds.
Weeding is what
this garden needs."

"No! No!" says the goat.
"No need for weeding.
Weeds are tasty.
Just start eating!"

"IT'S JUNE! IT'S JUNE!"
sing the beetles and slugs.
"You can't have a garden
without us bugs."

"We'll fly," sing the swallows,
"from garden to nests,
stuffing our babies
with plump, tasty pests."
"Pest? Who's a pest?"
asks a cabbage moth's son.
"Isn't this garden
for everyone?"

"There are peas," cries Daisy,
"on every vine!"
"I'm a great peapicker,"
says a porcupine.

The rabbits say,
"Now don't forget us.
We can help you
pick the lettuce."
"Honeyhoneyhoney,"
hum the bees.
"We spread pollen
with our furry knees."

"IT'S JULY!" chirp the bluebirds.
"We will harvest the cherries."
"We," say the bears,
"will gather the berries."

"And look!" says Daisy.
"The tomatoes are ready!
Let's make a sauce.
We'll have spaghetti!"

"There are carrots, beets,
and bumpy cucumbers,
and I counted zucchini
till I ran out of numbers…"

"And peppers," says a lizard,
"and collard greens,
string, lima, kidney,
and pinto beans!"

"IN AUGUST," raccoons croon,
"call evening or morn.
We'll come in a hurry
and pick all the corn."

Says the pig, "I am proud of my sensitive snout. It sniffs the potatoes and then digs them out."

"Like me," says the moon,
"the pumpkins are round.
I grow in the sky;
they grow on the ground.
By my gentle
silvery light,
shy visitors can
come at night.

"Some hop, some fly,
some nibble and run.
A garden is for everyone."

"SEPTEMBER!" cries Daisy.
"Come one and all
for a harvest picnic
to welcome fall.
What could be better,
as summer ends,
than feasting and dancing
with all our friends?

"Everything's ready,
ripe and sweet.
There's nothing to say,
except, 'Let's eat!'
And thank you, each,
for all you've done."
"Hooray for Daisy!"
says everyone.

"OCTOBER," sigh
the deer and crow.
They always are
the last to go,
sniffing the wind
for hints of snow.

Then Daisy hears
the wind's new song:
"Here comes winter,
cold and long."

And Daisy hears
the chickadee sing:
"Good-bye, garden,
until next spring!"